TICO

and the Golden Wings

Leo Lionni

Dragonfly Books —— New York

Many years ago
I knew a little bird
whose name was Tico.
He would sit on my shoulder
and tell me all about the flowers,
the ferns, and the tall trees.
Once Tico told me
this story about himself.

I don't know how it happened,
but when I was young
I had no wings.
I sang like the other birds
and I hopped like them,
but I couldn't fly.

TICO

and the Golden Wings

Luckily my friends loved me. They flew from tree to tree and in the evening they brought me berries and tender fruits gathered from the highest branches.

Often I asked myself, "Why can't I fly like the other birds? Why can't I, too, soar through the big blue sky over villages and treetops?"

And I dreamt that I had golden wings, strong enough

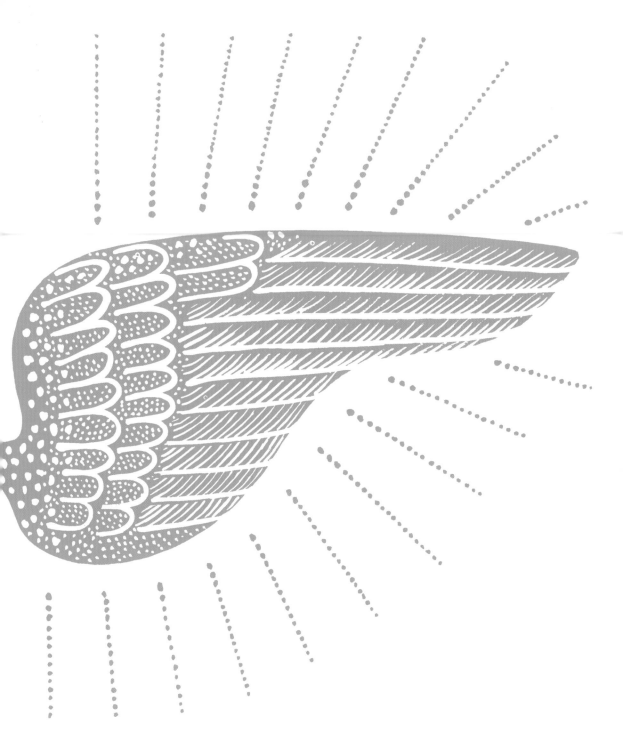

to carry me over the snowcapped mountains far away.

One summer night I was awakened by a noise nearby. A strange bird, pale as a pearl, was standing behind me.

"I am the wishingbird," he said. "Make a wish and it will come true."

I remembered my dreams and with all my might I wished I had a pair of golden wings. Suddenly there was a flash of light and on my back there were wings, golden wings, shimmering in the moonlight. The wishingbird had vanished.

Cautiously I flapped my wings. And then I flew.
I flew higher than the tallest tree. The flower patches below
looked like stamps scattered over the countryside
and the river like a silver necklace lying in the meadows.
I was happy and I flew well into the day.

But when my friends saw me
swoop down from the sky,
they frowned on me and said,
"You think you are better than we are,
don't you, with those golden wings.
You wanted to be *different.*"
And off they flew
without saying another word.

Why had they gone? Why were they angry?
Was it *bad* to be different?
I could fly as high as the eagle.
Mine were the most beautiful wings in the world.
But my friends had left me and I was very lonely.

One day I saw a man sitting
in front of a hut.
He was a basketmaker
and there were baskets
all around him.
There were tears in his eyes.
I flew onto a branch from
where I could speak to him.

"Why are you sad?" I asked.
"Oh, little bird, my child is sick
and I am poor.
I cannot buy the medicines
that would make him well."
"How can I help him?" I thought.
And suddenly I knew.
"I will give him one of my feathers."

"How can I thank you!" said the poor man happily.
"You have saved my child. But look! Your wing!"
Where the golden feather had been
there was a real black feather, as soft as silk.

From that day, little by little,
I gave my golden feathers away
and black feathers appeared in their place.
I bought many presents:
three new puppets for a poor puppeteer . . .

a spinning wheel to spin the yarn for an old woman's shawl . . .

a compass for a fisherman who got lost at sea . . .

And when I had given my last golden feathers
to a beautiful bride,
my wings were as black as India ink.

I flew to the big tree
where my friends gathered for the night.
Would they welcome me?

They chirped with joy.
"Now you are just like us," they said.
We all huddled close together.
But I was so happy and excited
I couldn't sleep.
I remembered the basketmaker's son,
the old woman, the puppeteer,
and all the others I had helped
with my feathers.
"Now my wings are black," I thought,
"and yet I am not like my friends.
We are *all* different.
Each for his own memories,
and his own invisible golden dreams."

About the Author

Leo Lionni, an internationally known designer, illustrator, and graphic artist, was born in Holland and studied in Italy until he came to the United States in 1939. He was the recipient of the 1984 American Institute of Graphic Arts Gold Medal and was honored posthumously in 2007 with the Society of Illustrators Lifetime Achievement Award. His picture books are distinguished by their enduring moral themes, graphic simplicity, and brilliant use of collage, and include four Caldecott Honor Books: *Inch by Inch*, *Frederick*, *Swimmy*, and *Alexander and the Wind-Up Mouse*. Hailed as "a master of the simple fable" by the *Chicago Tribune*, he died in 1999 at the age of 89.

Copyright © 1964, copyright renewed 1992 by Leo Lionni

All rights reserved. Published in the United States by Dragonfly Books,
an imprint of Random House Children's Books, a division of Random House, Inc., New York.
Originally published in hardcover in the United States by Pantheon Books, a division of Random House, Inc., New York, in 1964.
Dragonfly Books with the colophon is a registered trademark of Random House, Inc.

Visit us on the Web! www.randomhouse.com/kids
Educators and librarians, for a variety of teaching tools, visit us at www.randomhouse.com/teachers

The Library of Congress has cataloged the hardcover edition of this work as follows:
Lionni, Leo.
Tico and the golden wings; illus. by the author.
Summary: Illustrations and text tell about a bird without wings who is given golden wings by the wishing bird.
He loses his friends because they are envious. When he gives away his golden feathers, one by one, to help others,
he is given feathers like the other birds and they welcome him back.
ISBN 978-0-394-81749-1 (trade) — ISBN 978-0-394-91749-8 (lib. bdg.)
1. Fairy tales. 2. Birds—Stories. I. Title.
64018321
ISBN 978-0-394-83078-0 (pbk.)

MANUFACTURED IN CHINA
21 20 19 18 17 16 15 14 13 12

Random House Children's Books supports the First Amendment and celebrates the right to read.